I0619153

Home for an Amish Christmas

AMISH DREAMS ON PRINCE EDWARD ISLAND, BOOK 4

AMY GROCHOWSKI

For with God nothing shall be impossible.

Luke 1:37

Prologue

Elijah scrubbed at his closed eyelids with his two small fists, remembering he must wake early if he was to see his *mamm* before she left. But the light that penetrated his thoughts as he blinked his eyes open could only mean one thing.

Mamm left already.

Elijah mentally pushed back against the threat of tears. Seven-year-olds didn't cry.

He would be strong for his *mamm*. Maybe the man who claimed to be his father was no good, but Elijah would be good for his *mamm*. If he was a man instead of just a boy, they wouldn't have needed to come here.

He'd protect her. And she wouldn't have had to leave him here either, because he'd provide for her too.

Someday, he'd make sure his *mamm* never had to worry again.

With fists balled back up, Elijah shoved them deep into his mattress on either side of him and pushed out of bed, then walked to the window. Peering out, he could see the sun had already crested above the red-leafed tops of *Onkel Winston's* maple grove. Of course, Winston wasn't really his uncle. He was his mother's cousin who had moved to Prince Edward Island before Elijah was born.

Onkel Winston seemed nice—at least *Tante Mattie* never appeared afraid of her husband. And she was very kind. Still, sometimes folks put on an act for a while before their true self showed through, and Elijah had only been here for a week.

But his *mamm* wouldn't have brought him here to stay if she wasn't sure her cousin and his wife were good people, would she? *Nay*, he knew she would not. *Mamm* was brave to leave Pennsylvania and come here. If there was one thing Elijah knew for sure and certain, she'd done so for Elijah's sake—to keep him safe.

But who was going to keep *her* safe until she returned?

Seven-year-old boys didn't cry.

A puff of wind swayed the tree branches below his window, sending a shower of leaves to the ground. *Please watch over her, Jesus. She needs your help.*

Elijah stepped away from the window. He'd stay strong until she came back to visit. And they'd be together again after Christmas, she'd promised.

Chapter One

There was something oddly familiar about the woman seated in front of Mark Beller on the bus from Halifax to Charlottetown. He'd been distracted when she'd boarded after he did, and so he hadn't seen her face.

The ponytail that held her ash blonde hair tight against her head and cut just above the shoulder conflicted with the feeling that he knew her from among the Amish. Once, when she'd swung her legs into the aisle to make way for the passenger beside her to get to his window seat, he'd noted she wore running shoes and blue medical scrubs—definitely not Amish.

Mark leaned back against his own seat and closed his eyes to think. He had his Amish roots on his mind, was all. No doubt he'd never known the passenger in front of him.

For the next few weeks, he'd be with his family on Prince Edward Island for Christmas. This visit would make his longest single stretch at home since he left to join the Canadian armed forces seven years ago.

Already his equilibrium was off kilter. Off duty and out of uniform, he was without a sense of identity, too. He'd settle into civilian life, so he'd been told—like riding a bicycle. Only he'd never been a civilian before, not a regular one. Growing up Amish came with its own uniform and rules and governance, not much unlike the military in some aspects.

The irony made him chuckle. His Amish kin and friends wouldn't appreciate the comparison of their ways to military life.

But today, he was neither Amish nor military, except for his part-time job as a captain in the Reserves. Outside of that, he didn't belong anywhere exactly. And he had two weeks to figure out where and how he was going to start over with a new job and a new home.

One man alone didn't make much of a home, though.

Mark rubbed at his temples and blew out a slow breath. The bus slowed and the driver announced their impending stop at the University of Prince Edward Island in Charlottetown. The last bus from Charlottetown to Montague had run an hour earlier. From this point, he'd have to take a taxi to his parents' farm near Montague.

He'd been making do with public and military transport, but a top priority while home was finding his own vehicle—and not a horse and buggy. Mark preferred speed. He drew in a second deep breath and exhaled as the bus came to a full stop, then opened his eyes.

His focus settled on the now empty seat in front of him. Curious to catch a better glimpse of the woman, he scanned the aisle. She'd already made her way farther down toward the door. The bus lights were on, but her back was to him still, giving him no more clue to her identity than the same ponytail and now a small suitcase on wheels that she tugged behind her.

"Madame?" A male voice with a heavy French accent caught his attention. The passenger who'd been sitting beside her held up a brown bag. "Madame, your little boy's treats."

The gentleman projected loudly, but she didn't turn to acknowledge him.

"Here." Mark stood and held out a hand toward the man. "I'll catch her."

"Ah! Merci." Only then did Mark note the man stood with the help of a cane. He relinquished the bag to Mark and shrugged. "Would be a shame to leave her pastries."

Pausing only long enough to swing his backpack satchel across a single shoulder, Mark took two long strides in her direction, only to be stopped short by disembarking passengers spilling into the aisle. Mark angled his head anyway to keep tabs on her direction.

He was doing the right thing, nothing more, returning her forgotten treats. Yet something else propelled him. That nagging familiarity about her kept him curious enough to maintain this silly goose chase. Near the exit, he'd almost caught up when the doors opened. She was the first person off, never once looking back at him. And he was delayed as he allowed a family with small children to remain together ahead of him.

Outside in the open parking lot and still gripping the mystery woman's paper bag, Mark scanned the dispersing crowd by the dim light of the streetlamps, when he caught a glimpse of her profile at the entrance to a coffee shop—the same chain store as the logo printed on the bag in his hand. Undoubtedly, she was going to purchase donuts to replace those she'd left behind.

Mark followed her carrying the brown sack that didn't belong to him and a strange need to save an unknown woman the trouble of buying more donuts for her son.

Reaching into his pocket, he pulled out his phone to get a lift from Kari, Prince Edward Island's Uber equivalent.

Your driver, Sam, will arrive in 15-20 minutes in a white sedan. The text message flashed on his screen, along with a choice to accept or decline.

Certain that would be enough time to return the forgotten pastries into the hands of their rightful owner, Mark tapped to accept and pocketed his phone.

After looking through the short queue and an almost empty shop and seeing no one in blue scrubs, Mark pulled out a chair from a small table and sat where he could see the washroom exits. The long day of travel was wearing on his patience. His fingers drummed a steady rhythm on his bouncing knee. Finding a car was definitely a priority on this trip.

A woman in Amish dress emerged from the washroom, toting a wheeled case identical to that of the mystery woman. She was walking toward him, then stopped. Her eyes widened as he stood.

They both remained rooted in place, less than a few feet apart.

Ellen? The question echoed in his ears, though he hadn't said it aloud.

"Mark?" Her own question was barely audible.

It *was* her. Seeing Ellen again, after so long, jammed all his thoughts together like a massive pileup of railway cars behind a suddenly derailed engine.

"I... um...was waiting for someone. A woman..." He cleared his throat to gain better control of his voice. "She was in the washroom. Perhaps you saw her? A blond ponytail and blue scrubs. A nurse." He assumed that bit. Maybe she was a doctor or a phlebotomist, or a veterinarian. He had no idea, but he already felt too much the fool to explain.

"You were?" Her voice sounded unnaturally high-pitched, and she turned her head and coughed into her elbow.

"Do you need a drink?"

She shook her head. Still, he paused a moment to make sure until she seemed recovered.

"She left this on the bus." He held up the brown bag. "The passenger beside her said it was for her little boy. I was trying to return it."

"Oh." Ellen lifted her hand as though to take it, then dropped her arm back to her side. Not so fast that he didn't catch the glint of gold around her ring finger.

His assessment swept from her ring to the handle as she wrapped her fingers around and back down to the wheeled suitcase. Her luggage wasn't just identical to the other woman's. It was one and the same. And by Mark's best guess, a set of blue scrubs were now packed neatly inside. And no doubt, a blond ponytail was pinned beneath her head covering.

"You changed." And more than her clothes, since he'd last known her. Only he didn't say so. "You forgot something."

She looked at the bag from the donut shop, which had quickly slipped to the bottom of his concerns.

Obviously, she'd married and had at least one child. He'd known as much was likely... but he'd assumed that would be in Pennsylvania, not here. And why was she switching between Amish and non-Amish dress in public facilities?

He glared at her wedding band. "It doesn't match. You forgot to take it off. Wherever you're going dressed like... *that*... they don't wear jewelry.""

He expected her to hurry to remove the jewelry. Obviously she must in the playing of whatever game she was at. But instead of fumbling to remove the ring or offering a nonsense explanation, she raised her chin higher.

"Keep them." She waved at the bag in his hand. "I have to go."

Leaving him no time to ask any questions, she wheeled her case around and began walking away.

"Goodbye, Mark." She called over her shoulder.

Seven years hadn't changed as much as he thought, after all. Ellen had walked out of his life before and left him with more questions than answers.

The paper bag crunched under the pressure of his tightening grip as he fought the urge to go after her. How many times had he wished he'd done so before?

Too many.

But clearly, she didn't want him to follow her now, any more than she had the last time. And just like seven years earlier, he hated the vacuum she left behind.

How was it that this woman's absence could still leave him feeling empty? And once again paralyzed by an unexplainable desire to help her, yet absolutely no way to do so.

All those years ago, he'd done his best to help her get away from a terrible situation, even offered to marry her. But she'd run back home to the States. Mark had been helpless to do anything more for her, although held out some hope that the money he'd given her had helped.

That was then. This time, she was wearing a wedding ring. He'd never been told that she'd gotten married. Maybe he'd also held some ridiculous hope that she hadn't. But whatever was going on now, it was definitely none of his business.

He ought to be glad of it.

As soon as she was in the parking lot and out of Mark's sight, Ellen slowed her pace to catch her breath. Bumping into him again was a risk she'd taken in choosing to leave Elijah with her cousin, Winston, whose wife was Mark's twin sister. But Mattie often lamented how rarely her brother visited his family home on Prince Edward Island. Since Mark joined the military, Winston and Mattie had hardly ever seen him.

Besides being out of options, Ellen knew there was no more loving couple to care for Elijah in her absence. Her son was safe and loved with Winston and Mattie. The risk of seeing Mark again had seemed so low, and in the scheme of things her discomfort at the thought mattered little.

Until now.

Seeing him rattled her, and more than she'd have expected. All the what ifs, she believed long buried, came surging back to the surface of her emotions. And what terrible timing it was to be haunted by her past failures.

Why couldn't he have shown up after she got her life put back together? Why now, when she felt so much shame and embarrassment? And she'd run like a ninny, no different from before. As if she hadn't grown up at all. As if she hadn't lived a lifetime of regrets over the past seven years.

God, must I really face him again? Her heart groaned the question as she gazed heavenward.

She fumbled for her phone to call a taxi for the rest of the trip back to see Elijah. Her holiday wasn't off to a great start—not if Mark was headed in the same direction. He may not be, though. After all, there were plenty of other destinations that might've brought him to Charlottetown.

One could hope.

As she swiped at the screen of her phone, a bump to her back knocked her off-balance. She reached for her suitcase to catch herself, but there was nothing there. Stumbling slightly before securing her footing, she looked around for her luggage.

"Drop it!" An authoritative shout froze her in place. A thud, followed by the pounding of running feet, drew her attention to her left.

As a figure in a hoodie ran off, Mark bent down to retrieve her abandoned case. Earlier, she wouldn't have recognized Mark from behind. Although she'd instantly known his face, even in the scarcely lit bus. When she'd stood to get off, she saw him in the seat behind hers. His head had been reclined and his eyes shut. His once wild curly hair was cropped short, military-style, and had darkened from reddish blond to a chestnut brown. But she'd known him alright, and twice already today she'd attempted to get away from him, to no avail.

He turned, then, to face her. She noted his crisply ironed dress slacks and the starched white collar of his shirt, and she knew already his brown eyes remained as probing as ever.

Captain Beller, indeed. He fit the part, even out of uniform. Maybe too well. Her heart sped up as he came closer.

"Thank you." She reached for her case, regretting her earlier rudeness. Mark was a good man, but she wasn't prepared to answer his questions—especially about the ring on her finger. Although he was right, she needed to take it off.

Rather than pass Ellen's luggage to her, Mark nodded toward a white sedan parked by the curb. "I've already arranged for a ride. Why don't you take it? I'll get another."

The captain was still chivalrous. Her heart squeezed. Of course he was.

"We... um...," she hesitated, but may as well offer. It was inevitable at this point that she'd have to spend time with him.

"*Vass*?" What? He asked in their Amish dialect. Perhaps to ease her nerves—she doubted he ever spoke it much anymore.

"I expect we are headed to the same place." She explained, short of an outright invitation to travel together, and suddenly self-conscious of her heavy accent in English.

"Both going to New Hope, are we?"

"*Ya*. I'm on my way to your sister's house."

His expression gave her no clue whatsoever as to his feelings on that revelation. He simply glanced at her suitcase, which he had yet to pass back to her. And somehow, through it all, he still held onto the donuts for Elijah, too.

He nodded toward a waiting cab. "Well then, ladies first."

Chapter Two

S am, the driver taking them from Charlottetown to Montague, was friendly. He was young and enthusiastic. Ellen thought the ride might become a very talkative one. But when Sam's discussion turned to Ellen's Amish dress, Mark had interrupted.

Mark had been direct, not rude, sounding very much the captain in charge. Ellen understood why he felt Sam had stepped out-of-bounds, though she found his questions innocent enough. Still, it was no surprise when the remaining three-quarters of an hour were mostly silent.

Ellen didn't mind questions about Amish ways. Growing up in Lancaster, Pennsylvania, she was used to outsiders' curiosity. But she hadn't minded the quiet after Mark's interruption, either. And up front beside the driver, Mark appeared content to gaze out the window.

Ellen did the same to avoid staring at his side-profile, an up-close-and-too-personal reminder of her poor judgment. Pushing aside thoughts of what could have been, she focused on the joy of the upcoming two full days with her son Elijah.

Not only was it difficult for her to get a long weekend off for travel, the bus and taxi fares added up on her limited budget. In fact, she hadn't expected to get a full week off right at Christmas. Elijah was happily surprised, too. Their limited calls from Winston and Mattie's phone shanty just weren't enough.

This living arrangement couldn't last. She'd promised Elijah they'd only be separated through

Christmas. But she was no closer to a more suitable option than before.

In her heart, she knew that moving Elijah to Halifax would be no better for him, either. He belonged in the country, enjoying a childhood in the outdoors and surrounded by a community of people who loved him.

Her job in Halifax solved an immediate financial need in a moment of crisis. Thankful for a well-paying offer, she'd accepted the disadvantages of the location, believing something better would come along. Only she was still waiting for that answer to prayer.

But still, even if they ended up in a city, it was a far cry better for Elijah than anywhere Phineas Hertzler had a chance of taking Elijah away from her. Her work visa allowed them to remain in Canada for now. And God had blessed her efforts to obtain permanent residency on an express track, so far. She hoped that within the next six months, the government would approve her application. Indeed, God had watched over them through every step of this process.

Without a doubt, it was only by God's blessing the legal process had moved along so quickly in their favor. She could only trust and believe that He had the rest of the way planned ahead for them, too.

Near the village town of Montague, a light flurry of snow began to fall and continued as they made their way further south toward the small farming community the Amish called New Hope.

Elijah would be thrilled with the snow, she mused, as she slipped the wedding band off her finger and into the front pocket of her purse.

Breaking the silence, she asked Mark, "Will you stay until Christmas?"

"*Ya*," he switched into their Amish dialect again, explaining he'd come home for the following few weeks... maybe as long as a month. The last part seemed to be a reluctant divulgence.

The language shift offered some privacy. She wondered if he hadn't been more forthcoming than he wished, out of a hope she'd also explain herself. Where was she to begin?

"Did Mattie tell you that while I'm working in Halifax, she and Winston are watching Elijah... my son? It's only temporary. Until I can..." Even though the driver couldn't understand, she felt vulnerable and hesitated. "Until I can find a suitable place for us to live."

"*Nay*, she didn't tell me." Mark twisted his shoulders around enough to look back at her. He looked at her hands, folded in her lap, then back to her face and held her gaze. "What about your husband?"

"I don't have a husband." She refused to drop her head in shame, yet her lower lip trembled against her will. "I never married."

But Mark's expression didn't change to pity. Or judgment. His brown eyes probed hers for a brief interlude, and then he nodded. It was a barely perceptible nod. And maybe she only imagined a sort of approval behind it. For sure, she must've. The shadows and passing lights were fooling her. And yet her heart was bolstered, anyway.

"The ring," she continued in a near whisper, even though the driver couldn't understand, "is to keep away unwanted attention. I... I don't mean to be deceitful. It's just that... it makes things easier." So far from home and alone. Most people were well-intentioned in their match-making ploys. But others frightened her with their persistence. She felt like a target, and that flimsy piece of gold around her finger, the only jewelry she'd ever worn and the cheapest she could find, was a magic trick in keeping them away. "It works. Most of the time."

"Most of the time?" Mark turned back to face her again, as far as his seatbelt would allow. "I can help with the rest."

The offer surprised her, and her memory flashed back seven years to his offer to help her then. Her hand flew to her heart. But of course, he wouldn't make an offer like that now. She sucked in a breath.

"You don't train to serve King and Country without becoming well-acquainted in self-defense."

He'd switched to English, startling both Ellen and the driver.

"Easy now. Everything alright back there?" Sam was watching Ellen in his rear-view mirror. Was he concerned? She supposed Mark might've sounded threatening without the context of their conversation, but she'd understood his intent.

She smiled at the young man. Islanders were good folk in her experience. In the city, a total stranger wasn't likely to come to her defense so quick. "Everything is fine. He's only trying to be helpful."

"Well, I may not know much about the Amish, buddy," the driver switched his attention to Mark. "But even I know they turn the other cheek." He glanced back at Ellen. "Pacifists, right?"

Ellen nodded.

Mark growled and turned back around.

Sam had hit another nerve, this time an even bigger one with Captain Mark Beller. Silence returned. At least now, they were almost at Winston and Mattie's maple farm.

She could probably avoid more questions—but for how long? Thankfully, Mark was staying with his parents and not at his sister's house, but that would hardly make a difference. There'd be no avoiding Mark during this visit. And apparently not over the soon coming holiday, either.

Mark pressed the release button on his seatbelt. Ellen was already out of the vehicle and had her arms wrapped around the young boy who'd run to greet her. His short arms reached around her neck as she bent to kiss his blond head.

"Pop the lid, and I'll get her bags." Mark instructed the driver.

"Makes no difference to me, so long as I get paid." Sam leaned sideways to reach the lever to open the trunk. "You still going to that other address?"

Mark intended to see his *mamm* first and knew she'd be disappointed if he didn't arrive soon. But now that he was at his sister's house, he had to at least make a quick stop.

"I need to get down the road to the original destination. My parents are expecting me. But would you mind waiting a few minutes so I can say a quick hello to my sister first? I'll pay extra, of course."

Mark figured he could have been nicer to the young man to start off and rather expected him to say no, but Sam agreed to wait, and Mark hurried to get Ellen's bags for her.

Ellen looked back. Her eyes widened when she saw Mark had her bags. Her son was tugging her hand and pulling toward the house.

"Thank you." She mouthed the words before turning to go with her son.

Mark hadn't figured out what was going on exactly, but he was impressed by the fact she'd withstood immense family pressure to marry a well-off Amish man and raise her son by herself.

When he'd first met Ellen, he'd recognized her at once as a strong woman who could do whatever she set her mind to. And she was, until the surprise of a pregnancy shattered her confidence.

She'd come to Prince Edward Island to stay with her cousin, Lydia Yoder, and the church had hired her as their schoolteacher. She'd been happy among the Amish in New Hope.

And she'd been a breath of fresh air for Mark. He fell for her, hard and fast.

But when she'd discovered she was with child, things fell apart even faster. And it was the first he'd realized Ellen's reason for coming to Prince Edward Island had been to escape something secretly terrible at home.

Mark had been the only person in New Hope to whom she'd disclosed that she was expecting, before she left suddenly to go back home. Mark would've married her, covered a sin he never committed, and raised her child as his own. Instead, she'd chosen to go home to Lancaster. She'd run back to trouble, and Mark did, too, in the opposite direction to join the RCAF.

No wonder why. They'd been so young—nineteen and eighteen-year-olds—both totally unprepared for the real world. And he couldn't blame her for her refusal to jump the fence with him. At first, he'd been angry, sure, even heartbroken by the rejection. But he'd expected too much by asking her to raise a child outside of the faith. His support wouldn't have been enough, not even close.

And of course, he'd never foreseen a war in eastern Europe and how very absent he would have been from her life.

But now? How much had things changed... for them both?

"Mark!" His twin sister's voice brought him back to the present. Mattie was holding the door open for Ellen and her son. The kerosene lamp on the porch illuminated her face, revealing her happiness. "How *vunnerbar* to see you, *bruder*."

He dropped the bags on the porch and embraced his sister, then rested his hands on her shoulders and looked down into her eyes, wet with unshed tears. "Don't cry, Mattie. For heaven's sake, I've come home. Isn't that what you've been pestering me to do for ages?"

She wrapped an arm through his and pulled him toward the house. "*Kumm*, you must visit a little before you go home to *Mamm* and *Datt*. I have fresh maple donuts and hot cider."

"You always know just how to tempt me," he teased, "But the driver is waiting, and the weather is getting worse." He hated to see her disappointed. "I'll come over tomorrow as soon as *Mamm* lets me out of her sight."

"Which won't be any sooner than afternoon, I'm sure." She nudged him. "But go on. You're right. I'd be selfish to keep you from her a minute longer."

He hugged her.

"It's so *vunnerbar* to see you." Mattie gave him an extra squeeze before letting him go. "Make sure you come. As soon as we have a private moment, there's something I need to tell you."

"Don't worry, *schwester*. I'll be back." Mark tapped her chin and received the smile he hoped to get from her before he left.

The snowfall had intensified, and he hurried back to the waiting car.

He'd be back, for sure, and not only to visit his sister. Something had driven Ellen back to the island again, and he intended to discover what—or most likely—who it was.

Chapter Three

The comforting smell from a wood-burning stove awakened Ellen the next morning, as she opened her eyes in her cousin's simple guest room. Sunlight streamed through the window.

She'd overslept. No wonder, after all the tossing she'd done before falling asleep.

The past few months had been difficult, being away from Elijah and starting a new job in a new place, but she'd also been free of many of the worries she'd had in a long time. She was making progress toward a better life. Maybe more slowly than she'd hoped, as she still didn't have an answer for their future. Still, she'd found a deep sense of satisfaction in knowing she was finally getting closer.

Seeing Mark again tapped into long forgotten hopes. She'd fallen asleep by reminding herself that knights in shining armor didn't exist. By necessity or by choice—maybe some of both—making a new life for herself and Elijah was up to Ellen, alone.

And she'd have slept much better, if not for overhearing Mattie at the door with Mark the night before.

"When we have a private moment, there's something I need to tell you." Mattie had said to him.

A shiver ran up Ellen's spine. And she felt ridiculous for reacting that way. There were any number of private things a sister might wish to share with a brother.

Somehow, Ellen had to stop letting every hint of secrecy frighten her as if her own troubles haunted every whisper. As if every unknown was related to some threat to her or Elijah.

"Come see, *Mamm*." Elijah bounded into her room and stopped by the bed, still bouncing on his toes.

"What is it?" She pushed aside her thoughts, knowing she shouldn't be so paranoid, and took her son's hand. "What do you want me to see?"

"The kittens. Remember, you said in the morning. And guess what else?"

Ellen sat up on the edge of the bed. "I don't know."

"They're eyes opened." Elijah threw up his arms like a magician, revealing his greatest trick.

She pulled him to her in a bear hug. His cheeks were cold against hers. He must have run straight from the barn up to get her. Her heart melted, and she wished she hadn't slept so late. "That is *vunnerbar*, Elijah. I'll get dressed and be down just as fast as I can."

"If we're going to the barn, please wear a coat, Elijah." She called after him as he skipped out of the room.

After dressing quickly, she peered out the window to see almost a foot of fresh snow on the ground below and another memory of Mark sparked to life.

When she'd been a teacher for the Amish school in New Hope, Mark kept a sports car hidden from his family and the church, although she doubted it was truly much of a secret. But their many excursions around the island had been as discreet as possible—before he sold the car and gave her the money to get away from Phineas.

But the snow outside brought a distinct memory to mind of the evening when he'd taken her out in a sleigh after an early December snow. He'd taken her to the sweetest, quiet meadow where he'd built a lookout high in a maple tree. The stars had shone so brightly that night.

She pressed a hand against her heart, recalling the sound of their laughter against the wind, the redness of the noses and cheeks, the warmth of her hand in his, and the sweetness of his *mamm's* hot cocoa when they'd returned.

If knights in shining armor did exist, they'd look like the Mark Beller of her memories. She closed the door to those memories along with the bedroom door behind her and went to find Elijah.

There was no mystery in that. Elijah was already at the back door, waiting with her coat in his hand.

"*Danki*, Elijah." Taking the coat from him, she noticed Elijah's wrists stuck out several inches from the end of his sleeves. "*Ach*, you are growing too fast. I see you need a larger coat."

He smiled, likely at the notion that he was getting bigger, then shrugged. "I'll be fine. Let's go."

He was so enthusiastic. Watching him skip through the snow toward the barn, her heart squeezed at the thought of him cramped in a small apartment in Halifax.

But if they had no other choice, she'd make sure to visit New Hope and the Bellers whenever they could. Winston and Mattie assured her they would always be welcome.

Once again, she had to believe that some sacrifices were worth the cost of protecting Elijah from Phineas' influence. Coming here was the way the Lord had provided for her escape. *I'm trusting you, Gott. I cannot understand it all, but I am trusting You.*

Elijah looked back at her with eyes full of light and hope. Her child was trusting her, too. And she prayed every day not to let him down.

———

Mark had risen early to help his father and five brothers with the milking. Being in the military had kept him in the habit of getting up before the sun. In fact, the lifelong habits of dairy farming had done him plenty of favors when it came to service-life. Long days and hard work were natural for him. He couldn't say the same for most of the recruits who joined when he did. Their adjustment period had been considerably more painful.

But today, he wasn't a captain or even a lowly cadet. He was Herschel Beller's boy, helping alongside his brothers and doing the work their family had done for generations. And it wouldn't be too many years until the work passed to Mark's generation.

Michael was twenty-three. Myles and Martin weren't too far behind him, and the two youngest were almost out of school. Of course, Mark wouldn't be taking over the farm. He wondered which one of his brothers would. Their *datt* likely intended to wait for the youngest, Micah, to marry and take over the farm, and then he'd retire.

But for now, not much had changed, other than the expanding size of the dairy herd and the age of Mark's siblings. The work continued...

The dong of a bell rang loudly.

The familiar sound caused Mark's stomach to rumble. It seemed his *mamm* still used the mounted cowbell by the house to call them all in for a second breakfast—much heartier than the cereal and coffee they'd scarfed down before dawn.

Mark tossed a final load of manure and straw out of the barn, then stuck the pitchfork into a nearby hay bale.

She wouldn't have to call him twice. Nor anyone else—no surprise there—they all scuttled through the back door to the mudroom at the same time.

Seven men.

One wash basin.

And the pecking order remained the same, too. *Datt* washed up first.

No one dallied. The scent of warm bread and hot coffee, along with the sizzle of fresh sausage in the skillet, got them all to the table with heads bowed for prayer at a speed to impress the harshest of drill sergeants.

Some families ate in silence before conversing. Not the Bellers. Serving bowls passed, cutlery clattered, and at least three people talked at once throughout the meal.

"I miss this," Mark said to his *mamm*, while inhaling another bite of her fried potatoes.

Belinda Beller's eyes sparkled with pleasure. And Mark knew she'd be even happier if he shared a meal with them more often.

"Things will be different now, *Mamm*. I'll come to see you more often."

"Have you decided which job to take? The one in Halifax or Montreal?" Halifax slipped off her tongue with more approval in her voice than Montreal.

He'd be closer in Halifax, and he liked that idea, too. But the position in Montreal paid more.

"I have some time to figure it out. Neither company is making any final decisions over the holidays, so I have until after Christmas to give a definite answer." Sensing she disliked being put off more than his potential employers did, Mark went on, "I'll do my best to make sure and be home more. I promise."

She gave him a weak smile, as his brother Myles cut-in the conversation from across the table.

"Mark, what about you?"

"What about me?" Mark was lost to whatever Myles had been discussing.

"More snow is coming tonight, which means tomorrow will be a great day for sleigh-riding. And Mattie wants more greenery for the school Christmas program. I know you're probably not interested in an old fashioned, youth Singing tomorrow, but what about helping provide some sleigh rides? Michael says he'll do it."

"I said I'd do it if Mark does. Not the same thing."

Mark chuckled.

Michael was counting on Mark declining, so he could get out of it.

"Sure. I'll drive a sleigh full of rambunctious youngies, hyped up on hot cocoa. Got nothing better to do." Mark watched Micheal deflate. "Sorry, Mike. Guess you gambled and lost on that one."

A deep throat-clearing came from the head of the table.

Mark looked over at his *datt*. "Sorry. Just a figure-of-speech. I didn't mean any real gambling."

Anything Herschel may have said on the subject was drowned out by the excited whoops of the two youngest brothers.

"Who said you two could come along?" Martin teased them.

"Aw, c'mon. I'll be out of school in the spring. And it's not a real Singing. Besides, the greenery is for the school. Micah ought to be allowed as well." Mason always had his little brother's back. Mark loved that about him.

"Any brother of mine is welcome in my sleigh." Mark winked at Micah.

Michael coughed. "Have you seen your sleigh lately? You have some work cut out for you, if you plan to drive that thing tomorrow."

Actually, Mark hadn't thought that far ahead yet. "Any brother is welcome in *any* sleigh I'm driving," he corrected.

Mason leaned over toward Mark. "I'm sure Mattie and Mark would let you use one of theirs. They have two. Winston uses them for visitors to the farm in the winter."

"Thanks, bud." His little brother had just inadvertently given Mark a great excuse to go over to his sister's house—without being too obvious that he was there to see Ellen more than borrowing a sleigh.

His *mamm* leaned in from the other side. "*Ya*, you ought to go over soon—to see your *schwester*." The intentional emphasis on *schwester* wasn't lost on him.

His *mamm* knew Ellen was at Mattie's house. She was unashamedly matchmaking.

And as much as he probably should, Mark didn't mind. He wanted to see Ellen. Mostly because there was a mystery to solve, of course. Mark squeezed his *mamm's* hand and smiled at her.

"I'll go visit. Don't worry."

He downed a swig of coffee and filled his mouth with another hunk of sausage. For sure, he wasn't about to get into any talk about what else might be influencing his eagerness to visit his sister's house.

Chapter Four

"Hello, Winston." Mark greeted his brother-in-law, who answered the door when Mark arrived shortly after lunchtime.

"What's this? Since when does family knock at the front door before entering?" Winston gestured with mock offense, then smiled. "Maybe you'll be around more, now, and remember how we Amish do things."

His brother-in-law was a barrel-chested, hard-working man, not unlike the Bellers who earned their muscle on the dairy farm. Winston, though, had built his strength in his family's construction business before he'd moved to the island and married Mattie. Now, he and Mattie maintained a growing maple farm, harvesting and producing quality syrup as well as a sweet shop that attracted visitors year round, but especially during the holidays.

"Ah, you still have your American sense of humor, I see. Though I have to say, Winston, you're getting a Canadian accent. We'll have you trained right soon enough."

"Good one." Winston chuckled. "Mattie is in the kitchen. She started some hot cider as soon as she saw you coming."

Mark slipped out of his coat, careful not to drip the melting snow on the floor. "The snow picked up again, all of a sudden."

"*Ya*, sure did. I just came in from the barn." Winston took Mark's coat. "Gotta hang mine up, too. Ellen is still outside with Elijah. He's taken on the challenge of fattening up the runt of a new litter of kittens. I think they're bottle-feeding it now."

Small talk filled the gaps of conversation as Winston washed his hands, then joined Mattie and Mark at the table. As her husband reached for a donut, Mattie poured him a mug of hot cider like the one Mark sipped.

"I was about to tell him." Mattie said to Winston, "About the visitor we've had."

"Visitor—that's a polite way to put it." Winston's brows drew together, creating a pinched line on his forehead. He looked at Mark and began where Mattie had left off. "He's gone, but a fella from Lancaster was snooping around with questions about a boy who fit Elijah's description. Course, folks here didn't tell him much of anything."

Mark felt Mattie's hand rest on his forearm before she continued what her husband had left off.

"It's going to spook Ellen when she finds out." She glanced out the window in the barn's direction. "Can't say as I blame her. But our people will protect her. Joel promised her, and Joel never says something he doesn't mean."

Joel Yoder was a minister in the New Hope district Amish church and his character was well known. Mark even knew from personal experience that Joel to be a man of his word.

Mark thought back to the days just before he left the community and how Joel had shown him both patience and mercy. If Joel felt Ellen required the church's protection, Mark had to wonder why? "So who exactly are we protecting Ellen from?"

"We?" Mattie smiled at him, and too late, Mark realized he'd included himself in the group.

"You know what I meant." Mark bit into a donut, acting as though his word choice had no meaning. *Out of the abundance of the heart, a man speaketh.* He swallowed, afraid to ponder the implications of the proverb which his memory dredged up at the worst possible moment.

A screen door slammed shut, and he knew he'd been saved from further scrutiny by his observant twin—at least temporarily. Undoubtedly, she'd press him further about it later. His family all wanted to know his intentions now that he was a civilian again.

As footsteps sounded through the front room toward the kitchen, he expected to see either Ellen or Elijah. Instead, a snow-covered young woman stepped into the kitchen doorway and leaned against the frame.

Her red-hair curled freely in all directions with no prayer *kapp* in sight. She was pale, ashen really, and didn't say a word.

"Samy?" Mattie hurried toward the girl Mark now recognized as Joel and Lydia Yoder's oldest child.

Mark stood, too. Something was amiss. Her eyes were glassy, which he noticed just before her lids slowly closed over them. She slumped, and Mark barely caught her before she hit the floor. As he eased her down, his palm met with a warm sticky substance on the back of her head.

"She's bleeding." Mark told his sister.

"Get Ellen." Mattie instructed Winston, who raced for the back door.

"And call 9-1-1." Mark hollered loud enough for his brother-in-law to hear on the run.

Samy startled at the nearness of his voice and moaned. Her eyes fluttered open. And Mark was encouraged to see her respond. At least she was conscious.

"Rachel is coming," she said.

Mark stifled a groan as the flow of blood seeped through his fingers. They needed a paramedic. Rachel was the local vet tech.

"Do you have a clean dishtowel?" He asked his sister, who hurried to retrieve one for him.

He was pressing the clean cloth against the wound and cradling Samy's head in both of his hands while also attempting to keep her spine straight, when Ellen returned.

Ellen took one glance at Samy and turned to Mattie. "My bag?"

"In the living room." Mark motioned with his head toward the other room and Mattie left quickly to get it for Ellen.

"She's lost a lot of blood, I think." Mark said quietly as Ellen squatted beside him on the floor. "Did Winston go to call emergency services?"

She nodded a confirmation as she felt Samy's pulse. "Keep her awake."

He knew not to allow a possibly concussed person to sleep and spoke softly to Samy while Ellen rummaged through her bag.

"Why is Rachel coming?" The question had been on his mind, and Ellen also looked to Samy for the answer.

"Amazon is hurt." Samy's eyes filled with tears and Mark felt an aching pain for the girl. Amazon was Joel's Morgan mare, an exquisite horse and especially important to Samy.

"Find out what happened," Ellen quietly instructed him before asking Mattie for a bottle of peroxide, some pillows, and a warm blanket.

So Mark continued with questions, hoping to keep Samy awake and also learn what had happened.

"I called her from the phone shanty. Rachel said she would come if I promised to come inside. She made me leave..." Samy began to cry.

"Shhh..." Mark slid one of his hands from behind her head and stroked the curls back from her forehead. "Rachel will take care of Amazon. Now, we must let Ellen take care of you. Okay?"

"Could you try to drink some warm tea?" Ellen asked, likely in hopes of rehydrating her after the blood loss and to help the poor girl's shock.

Samy sat up so quickly Mark almost lost the pressure he'd been maintaining against the back of her head. She waved frantically in an indiscernible direction. "The man."

Ellen suddenly froze. The fear on her face hit Mark's heart like a blow.

"What man?" Mattie asked softly.

"In the car...who will help that man?"

The three adults looked at one another in unison. Mattie's mouth opened in surprise. Ellen's fearful expression changed to concern, and the tension in her posture relaxed.

"If a car was involved, Winston needs to let the emergency responders know." Mark told his sister, wondering why the revelation of a car on the scene had relieved Ellen's growing tension.

Samy's initial mention of a man's presence had definitely spooked her.

"I'll go tell Winston to let them know another person might be injured." Mattie disappeared too fast for Mark to offer the use of his cellphone. So instead, he gently coaxed Samy back into a prone position and held her head.

"Winston will call for help," Mark tried to reassure her. If she moved suddenly again, he was afraid the bleeding would restart.

Whatever had worried Ellen a minute earlier, she was no longer showing it. As well as any medical professional might, she checked Samy's hips and legs before elevating her feet on the pillows, then reached for the blanket Mattie had left behind. As he brought the cover up to Samy's waist, Ellen took the girl's hands and asked her to squeeze.

"*Goot*, Samy. You have a firm grip. The same on both sides." She patted the smaller hands as he placed them on the girl's abdomen, then wrapped the blanket all the way to Samy's shoulders.

Mark watched as Ellen flashed a small light into Samy's eyes. Both pupils dilated normally. He exhaled with relief. The military taught him enough first aid to understand that the equal dilation and the equal hand strength were positive. And even minor head injuries could bleed a lot. Perhaps Samy wasn't hurt as badly as it first appeared.

"I don't see any other obvious injuries." Ellen said as she leaned back on her heels. "No obvious broken bones. Of course, I can't see internally. And I don't have a blood pressure cuff." She was so close Winston could smell the lilac perfume of her shampoo as she put a hand on his shoulder. "You're doing a great job. Keep her calm and awake. If you scoot behind her, you can rest her head on your legs to maintain the pressure... your arms are going to get tired. I'll hold her head while you move."

She leaned across him to hold the towel so he could shift his position. "Can you see?" she asked. "Has it bled through?"

He looked carefully under the towel. "Not that I can tell."

Her lips curved even higher than before in a hopeful smile. He, too, was relieved by yet another good sign.

Once he had Samy resettled, Ellen stood. "Probably best we don't disturb the wound. They can determine what to do about that when they come."

He looked up at her. "You're a nurse?"

She nodded. "I'll get her some fluids... some tea. Hopefully, the EMT's will be here soon."

He wanted to ask how she'd managed nursing school, but the story would have to wait. When Mark looked back at Samy, her eyelids were closing.

"You're a very brave girl." Mark spoke into her ear, hoping to keep her awake. He tried to think of something to get her talking. Horses, he knew, were her favorite subject, but right now that might only upset her. What did a thirteen or fourteen-year-old think about? "You know, the boys will all be impressed by how brave you have been today."

"*Sie sind verruckt.*" She called him crazy, and Mark tried not to laugh. "I don't care what the boys think."

She sounded so definitive on the matter, but Mark discovered he had hit the jackpot because Samy had quite a lot to say, considering how little she claimed to care about boys.

"I think this will be cool enough for her." Ellen returned with a teacup and smiled down at Samy. "I added extra sugar for you."

Mark reached for the cup only to realize his fingers were stained from holding Samy's bandage.

"Get away!" A boyish voice demanded, drawing Mark's attention the other way. "Don't you touch my *mamm.*"

From the entrance to the kitchen, Mark's sister barely caught Elijah by the back of the shirt in time. He'd been about to plow straight into Mark. His arms were still swinging as Mattie yanked him back against her and held him tight. A woman didn't grow up with six brothers without learning a trick or two about how to handle a boy.

The dark suspicion in Elijah's eyes was something Mark had seen before, though overseas in the eyes of refugees, never from one of his brothers. Mark and Mattie's siblings hadn't experienced the danger that gave a child reason to look that way at another person.

Mark slowly eased his hand down to a neutral position and maintained eye contact with the boy, willing him to understand he posed no threat. The boy stopped swinging, but his glare remained intense.

"Elijah," Ellen's voice drew the boy's attention to herself. "Samy is hurt. Mark is Mattie's sister. He's a good man who is helping her."

Ellen walked around to her son and put a hand on his shoulder, much as she'd done to Mark earlier, and he wasn't sure how he felt about that. For sure, the way she handled her distraught child was admirable. Still, he made a mental note not to attribute more from her touch than she intended. After all, she'd just calmed a small child in the same manner, and maybe the connection he'd felt earlier hadn't held the meaning he'd felt buzz through him at her touch.

She had called him a good man, though, a compliment he better not read into, either.

"I need your help, too." She spoke kindly but firmly to her son, who didn't immediately comply or rebel.

Beneath a stern brow, Elijah's sharp eyes watched Mark and assessed Samy. He was determined not to be fooled, Mark thought. Experience had toughened this boy beyond his years. Mark hid the pity that gripped his heart. Elijah wouldn't like to see it.

Then, as an obedient son ought, Elijah nodded to his mother. She sent him to haul in firewood—a task to keep him busy and out of the kitchen. The whirr of emergency sirens already filled the air. The room would soon become crowded with paramedics, and most likely, Samy's parents were also on their way.

Nothing about this visit was turning out how he'd imagined. He was trained in military intelligence, yet he'd come home ignorant of some important details. How had he not known that Ellen's son was staying with his own sister?

Mattie wouldn't have kept news like that from him unless asked expressly. And Mark suspected that was precisely why he hadn't been told. Of course, he hadn't thought to ask, either. He'd expected everything to be the same. Just as it always was among his Amish family.

He'd been wrong.

Civilian life, at least for the next few weeks, may not be as mundane as he'd been prepared to endure. Mark enjoyed a puzzle, and Ellen presented one he never had been able to solve.

Maybe this time, he finally would.

And he'd be more careful not to conclude with a shattered heart this time.

Chapter Five

Snow, the heavy wet kind best for snowballs, topped everything in sight like smooth white cream—except for Elijah's footprints along the pathway from the woodshed to the back door. After quickly dumping a few inches, the snowfall had lessened. Still, Elijah continued back and forth with armloads of wood as his *mamm* had asked.

He'd already carried several loads to the house since the ambulance had arrived. So on this trip, he peaked around the corner into the kitchen to see what was happening. The room was full of people. The chatter wasn't loud, not the same as a visiting

Sunday when lots of people were talking and laughing at once, filling the house like loud music. *Nay*, this was quieter, as if everyone was taking care to speak softly. And yet so many spoke at once that nothing was easy to understand.

Joel Yoder was tall, which made the local Amish minister, also Samy's *datt*, easy to recognize even with his back turned to Elijah. Samy's *mamm* held her daughter's hand and whispered into Samy's ear. He imagined Lydia must be saying that everything was going to be alright.

Elijah hoped so. Samy was nice, the way he reckoned a big sister would be if he had one.

Most of the others were dressed in medical uniforms, some like his *mamm*, and others in heavy coats with reflective stripes. Firefighters, maybe, who'd have come because of the car accident. They were usually the first to arrive in an emergency.

He was thinking how he might become a firefighter one day, when his gaze connected with the other non-Amish man in the room—the one his *mamm* had assured him was there to help. He had kind eyes, looking back at Elijah both caring and strong. Elijah's heart felt a strange and unexpected connection with the man. Trust. That's what he felt. His *mamm* was right. This was a good man.

"Not much longer," the man said to him.

Reassured, Elijah returned to his task. After all, the best way to be helpful was to obey his *mamm*. Only there were a new set of footprints outside. Positive the man-sized boot prints weren't there before, curiosity dragged him away from his wood-gathering task. Closer to the trail, he saw the tracks came from around the house and headed to the barn. Sure that he'd brought in enough firewood already, the trail to the barn was too irresistible not to follow.

"*Onkel* Winston, can I help you?" Elijah hollered before he noticed things in the barn seemed oddly quiet. Winston was definitely not there.

No more that five steps inside, a wet tongue licked his ear from the side. "*Ach*, Beulah." Eli wiped his ear with the back of his hand, then faced his favorite Jersey cow. "I don't have any treats. Where's Winston?"

Beulah nudged his shoulder, trying to reach into his pockets, making him laugh.

"I told you I don't have anything." He reached for a pitchfork, thinking to get her a bit of alfalfa hay.

She bellowed an unpleasant kind of sound.

"Be patient, won't you?" Elijah scolded.

He turned and noticed a shadowy figure at the other end of the barn. He couldn't make out who it was, aside from being a man.

Beulah bellowed again.

The man was too big to be Winston. And whoever it was, Beulah didn't like him.

Elijah gripped the pitchfork handle until the splintering wood dug into his palm.

"Hello, Elijah." The grating whine of that horrible voice he'd heard before triggered a rash of goosebumps along both of Elijah's arms.

Don't come any closer, Elijah wanted to say to the man who claimed to be his father, but his mouth wouldn't move and his voice must've frozen over. Instead, he held the pitchfork like a spear, daring him to come any further.

Elijah refused to believe this man was his father. Maybe the bully understood he meant to use the pitchfork if necessary because he backed up a step. Only he didn't leave, and Elijah was torn about whether or not to run and warn his *mamm*. As long as he kept the man in the barn, Elijah's *mamm* was safe. But how long could they stand here, silently staring at each other?

———

Once the paramedics arrived, Mark remained in the background, allowing them to do their jobs while he kept a watch on Elijah from the window. Ellen's boy sure had a strong work ethic for a seven-year-old. Even for an Amish kid, Mark thought this one worked too much like an adult and not nearly enough like a child.

If Mattie hadn't mentioned a troubling stranger had been about asking questions about Elijah, Mark might not have paid attention when a man he didn't recognize walked around to the back side of the barn. After all, Mark wasn't home often enough to know who belonged and who didn't, but when Elijah wandered to the barn rather than returning to the woodshed, he feared something was amiss.

As he was no longer needed to help with Samy, Mark eased his way around the busy workers filling the room. He was about to leave the same way Elijah had earlier when a tap on the shoulder stopped him at the door.

"You saw him too?" It was Joel, and Mark turned to answer.

"I don't know who I saw, but it worries me that Elijah followed after him." Mark kept his voice low, attempting not to alarm Ellen.

Joel nodded toward the door, as if to say they ought to continue their discussion outside. They stepped out together and Joel closed the door behind them.

"I don't want to leave Samy and Lydia long, but I also need to make sure Phineas knows that I know he's come lurking about again."

So, the man's name was Phineas. Mark made a mental note of the name and rapidly developed a plan. "How about you say what needs to be said, and then take Elijah back to the house with you? I'll get this Phineas character off the property."

"Peacefully."

Mark agreed with a nod. He wasn't a hot-head like he'd been in his youth.

"Peacefully is always the better way." *When given the option*, but he wasn't here to debate that difference of opinion with Joel Yoder.

Right now, they both just wanted to make sure that Elijah wasn't in danger, although he realized he didn't actually know what kind of threat this man posed or why.

"Is this Phineas guy dangerous? Or is he just causing trouble?"

Joel grunted in a wordless, non-committal way.

"Look, I'm not asking you to break any confidences. I just need to know something before we go in there. If you're willing to leave Samy and Lydia's side at a time like this, then this Phineas person is obviously bad news."

Not to mention the clues both Ellen and Elijah had unknowingly given that at one time they'd been in danger from someone. Mark didn't need to be a genius to reckon Phineas was a large part of their trouble.

"He won't be meaning to do any *goot*." Joel's dark eyes set in a determined gaze toward the barn. "I'll go in the barn's front door. You come around the back. From there, we follow your plan. I get Elijah back to the house. You get Phineas as far away as you can manage." Joel straightened his shoulders. "We can talk more later."

"Fair enough." Mark agreed and walked on ahead.

Mark double-timed around the barn, attempting to enter the far-side as close as possible to Joel's entrance from the front. As he came around to stand just outside the wide opening, the sun broke through the clouds from the perfect angle to illuminate the inside.

Elijah stood stock-still with a pitchfork aimed straight ahead like a javelin aimed at the man's head. Elijah squinted toward Mark. Mark shook his head and pressed a finger to his lips. The child instinctively understood not to give him away and looked away silently.

Phineas remained turned with his back to Mark, as Joel entered the barn and walked toward Elijah. Mark guessed Phineas was at least as tall as Joel, maybe taller, though his bad posture made it difficult to tell.

Phineas wobbled slightly. He must have seemed a formidable size to seven-year-old Elijah, but Mark breathed a sigh of relief. The man was in no condition to put up a fight. Although, you never could tell what strength lay within an intoxicated man.

Mark remained on guard, waiting for Joel to take the lead. In a few long strides, Joel was directly behind Elijah, placing a hand on the boy's shoulder in a pastoral manner.

Elijah looked up at Joel and gave no resistance when he took the pitchfork and set it aside.

"Phineas." Joel's voice resonated with the authority he held in the community as a minister. "Your welcome here has run out."

Phineas lunged forward clumsily, but Mark outpaced him to gain a firm grip on the man's upper arms from behind.

"Looks like you were about to take a tumble." Mark stated casually for Elijah's sake, as if the man were clumsy rather than a menace, but he didn't let go. If anything, Mark tightened his grasp. "I'll just help you stand here. We wouldn't want you to fall."

Sensing the rage building in the man under his hold, Mark nodded at Joel, hoping he understood it was time to get Elijah out. "I've got this."

Joel gently turned Elijah around to leave, and Phineas jerked toward them. Unable to release himself from Mark's stronghold, Phineas growled instead.

"He's my *sohn*. You can't keep him away from me."

"I'm not!" Elijah spun around. "I'll never be like you. Ever!"

The sorrowful sound of Elijah's agony stabbed a sharp pain through Mark's heart. He realized that this man very well could be the boy's father. A memory of the same tortured look on Ellen's face long ago at the mention of the man who fathered her child momentarily stunned him.

Mark's grip loosened, and Phineas slipped from his hold. But before Mark even needed to react, Winston entered the barn with a police officer at his side.

Phineas halted, then turned to run but plowed into Mark.

Although he felt as if he'd been pummeled by a demolition ball, Mark remained sturdy enough to stop Phineas from getting away. And then faster than Mark could catch his breath, the officer pulled out her handcuffs and slapped one side around the wrist nearest to her.

"You will need to come with me to answer questions about the accident which occurred just down the road." Her no-nonsense tone sobered Phineas into standing straight.

Joel stepped up and nodded at the cuffs. "I'm sure you won't need those. Phineas will go peacefully and answer your questions."

Anger burned behind Phineas'eyes, but he nodded in agreement.

If she agreed, Mark determined to go along to make sure Phineas kept his end of the bargain, but she ordered him to put the other hand behind his back before cuffing that wrist, too.

"Sorry," she said, "You shouldn't have tried to run."

Good decision.

No sooner had the thought crossed his mind than Mark saw Elijah watching Phineas go. The child was shaking. Instinctively, Mark wrapped an arm around the boy's shoulder, and half-expected him to pull away. After all, Elijah didn't know him. He ought to have let Winston or Joel comfort him.

Only Elijah didn't pull away.

Mark took heart and bent down to eye level. When those tender brown eyes, so like Ellen's, peered back at him, Mark couldn't help but embrace her son in a tight hug. As Elijah's arms wrapped around his neck, Mark picked him up. He'd carried children before, but he'd never felt a connection the way he did now.

And he didn't have a name for it. Except love.

Chapter Six

The previous day's weather left behind a half-foot of snow when all was said and done. Now the Sunday sun shone brightly in an absolutely clear blue sky as the Amish of New Hope made their way to Noah and Rachel Detweiler's farm for worship. The roads were slushy with melting snow, but the rolling hills of farmland were a welcome sight to Mark.

He may no longer be truly Amish, but in his heart Mark still loved the peace that came with acre after acre of traditionally farmed land. He'd convinced his *mamm* to ride with him in the sleigh to service this morning, while the rest of his brothers loaded up in the long-wagon with their *datt* and traveled by the main road.

Convincing his *mamm* hadn't been difficult. He felt a tad guilty about how little time he'd spent with her due to all the unexpected chaos the day before. And she was clearly thrilled that he'd chosen to attend their worship services. Belinda Beller loved all six of her sons, and still she knew how to make each one feel like her favorite.

Mark felt a smile spread across his face. This sleigh ride to church was his moment with her, and he'd waited a long time for it. So had she.

She patted his knee briefly before sliding her hand back under the blanket across her lap. "Wait until you see what Noah has done with the Detweiler farm. Not only is he rescuing horses but *kinner* as well with his horse therapy. Samy practically lives over there nowadays, helping with the horses. Yesterday's accident must have been a terrible shock for her."

"She was in shock at first, but she bounced back as fast as any well-trained soldier. That girl's made of tough stuff. I don't think that fall will hold her back long. And Rachel says Amazon will make a full recovery. The young driver handled his vehicle well, all things considered. It could have been far worse. He's doing just fine, too."

"Your *bruder* was fit to be tied. Don't you say anything to him, but I think he has feelings for Samy. He'd deny it, of course, say he'd be concerned no matter who it was. But a *mamm* knows."

"Myles, you mean? I noticed he was especially sullen last night. But he's too old for Samy. And the others are too young."

"Four years is a giant age difference right now, maybe. But before you know it, several years will pass and it won't be anything unusual... when she's twenty and he's twenty-four. It's a long wait but..." She lifted a shoulder and tilted her head to the side. "Only *Gott* knows, of course, but Myles has grown into a constant, steady young man. So we will see what happens."

"Don't worry, *Mamm*. I won't say a word." Myles likely thought no one could guess his feelings and would be mortified to know their *mamm* had sniffed him out. If she was right, and Mark had no doubt she was. She knew her *kinner* better than they knew themselves.

"You know something about waiting, though, don't you, *sohn*?" A hint of mischief in her voice gave away her meaning.

"I wouldn't exactly say I've been waiting... more like detoured."

"And yet, seven years later, here you and Ellen both are again. Don't you think maybe *Gott* had a hand in the timing?"

"I admit, I've wondered." Lost some sleep thinking about it, too. And it wasn't just his old feelings for Ellen tugging at his heart. Elijah had ambushed his heart and soul in one big hug. He'd heard parents say how they instantly feel in love with their children. He thought that was only biological. Apparently not.

Mark wasn't going to reveal any of those sentiments right now. The worst thing he could do to his *mamm's* tender heart was get her hopes up that he might return and join the Amish.

"And..." His *mamm* didn't give up easily.

And Mark knew she deserved more of an answer. "Ellen rejected me before, you know. And you must also know it was because of the path I've chosen. That hasn't changed, *Mamm*." As far as he could tell, Ellen had one foot in the English world, but only barely, and out of necessity. "Ellen is still Amish."

His mamm's breath caught, and she looked away momentarily.

Switching the reins to one hand, Mark placed the other on top of the blanket and squeezed his mother's hand.

"I love my family. And I am thankful for the faith and love you gave me, but I cannot be Amish. Leaving the Amish wasn't *all* my choice. I'd be awfully arrogant to think it was my own will alone that has led me to where I am now. God has given me a different path to follow. So, I must."

His *mamm* swiped a tear from her cheek.

"I'm sorry." His vision blurred slightly. Hurting his *mamm* was the worst thing he'd ever done.

"*Nay, sohn.*" She patted his knee and let her hand rest there. "I am grateful that you are honest with me. And I am pleased that you are doing your best to follow *Gott* wherever He takes you." Her voice wavered, and she paused before continuing. "More than any of my children, *Gott* has used you to stretch my faith. That is not a bad thing, you understand. Just hard."

Ellen was about to give Elijah another push on the swing when he dropped his legs and dragged his feet to a stop. She cringed at the amount of mud she'd be cleaning from those shoes before he went to school the next day.

But... at least she would get to see him off to school. And Rachel mentioned before service that a local pediatrician's office would soon be advertising an open position for a nurse. If that panned out, she may not need to leave Elijah at all for much longer. Finding a house here would be much better than taking Elijah to the city.

"He's just over there, *Mamm*. Can't we go talk to him now?" Elijah pointed across the playground toward Rachel and Noah's barn, where Mark leaned back against the fence.

He had one foot on the ground and the other propped on a lower fence rail. His arms were crossed with one elbow bent so that his hand reached his chin. Was he thinking or staring?

Ellen's heart stuttered when his eyes met hers. Even so far away, she knew he'd seen her.

"Don't point." She looked down at Elijah. He'd prattled on about Mark non-stop since the incident with Phineas. "What is it you want to say to him so badly?"

"*Danki*, of course. I thought you would tell him... but you didn't."

Ellen winced. Her son often sounded more like an adult than a child. "There was so much happening, Elijah. I was taking care of Samy."

Elijah looked unconvinced but didn't talk back. He wasn't a smart-mouth—for which she was thankful. Still, she knew he had a point. If she'd tried, she could have thanked Mark for his help. While she didn't know what Phineas' intentions had been in Winston's barn, she knew he'd been intoxicated. And bad things happened when Phineas drank too much.

"You're right." She ruffled Elijah's hair. "We should thank him properly."

In a flash, Elijah jumped from the swing and ran in Mark's direction. Mark noticed and began walking toward them both when Noah Detweiler came from the other direction and stopped to speak with Mark.

Elijah, of course, didn't care and ran straight up to the two men.

Ellen followed more slowly. She'd be rude to interrupt. Or really, she dreaded facing the reality that Mark now knew about Phineas—revealing to him how desperately stupid she'd been in her youth. So as Noah spoke to Mark, she waited a few feet back, looking at her feet, or the pasture, or anywhere but at Mark's face.

Elijah had no such inhibition. He stood, somewhat antsy, close to Mark's side, looking up at him as though he were a hero.

Mark glanced down at her son, then moved his hand from his chin to rest lightly on top of Elijah's shoulder. Ellen sucked in a breath at the tenderness of the sight and looked away to fight against the threat of tears behind her eyes.

Pull yourself together. She pretended to watch the other children now playing on the swing-set, as the men's conversation continued.

"I heard you came by car this time." Noah chuckled, though Ellen couldn't imagine what was funny about that. "Last time I saw you, you were pushing a broken-down motorcycle."

"Yeah, I had to give that one up a long time ago."

"Well, I'm ever grateful to that old clunker for getting you to me—or close enough—that day. The letter you delivered from Rachel changed my life. I owe you for that. And I've always wondered what made you care enough to bring it in person."

Ellen heard the scuff of a boot against the ground and got the nerve to look back at Mark. He always kicked the ground when he was nervous or shy about something.

"It seemed like Rachel and your *datt* were both hoping for a second chance. I don't who for. For you, for her, for him? But whatever the case, I hoped that maybe someday I'd be given a second chance too."

Mark looked around Noah, directly at Ellen, and her breath hitched.

Ellen wasn't sure exactly how or why Noah stepped away from them, but she found herself right in front of Mark with only Elijah between them. Her breaths became shallow and her heart beat too fast.

A second chance... how often had she dreamed of one?

All those years ago, she would have joined Mark in the English world, but for being with child. Maybe she should have. If Mark was the only father her son ever knew... if the outside world was the only one he'd ever experienced, maybe it would have all worked out.

But she hadn't. Elijah was happy being Amish... and Phineas had figured things out.

"Mark..." She had so much to say. Yet nothing to say. Even if Mark had been implying that he'd give her a second chance, how could she take it?

From where she was now, being with Mark was an impossible leap—even more than it had been the last time.

"*Danki.*" Elijah filled in the silence. "That man is not my *datt*, you know. No matter how much he says so, I know in my heart that he isn't. He hurt my *mamm*, and now you showed him he can't do that again."

The unshed tears Ellen held back earlier surged to the surface again, and she looked down, as speechless as ever.

Mark was kneeling at Elijah's level, and she was relieved he hadn't seen her tears.

"There are a lot of good people here to make sure you and your *mamm* are protected. And I will always do what I can to be one of them. But never forget, your Father in Heaven will always be with you, even when none of us can be. Remember what Joshua said before the Israelites took the land God promised them?"

Elijah shook his head.

"*'Be strong and of a good courage; be not afraid... for the Lord thy God is with thee whithersoever thou goest.'* Can you remember that?"

"I will." Elijah nodded his head eagerly. "And when Jesus was born, the angel told the shepherds not to be afraid. That's my part of the Christmas program. I had to *rememberize* it."

Mark grinned at the made-up word, and Ellen bit her lip not to laugh as Elijah ran back to the play set.

"Thank-you. And not only for yesterday, but for what you did just now."

"I'd do more... if I could... if you'd allow me." He stepped closer, paused briefly, and continued with purpose before she could respond. "I was just talking with Noah about a car he thinks is for sale. But for today, it's sleigh riding. And nothing would make me happier than if you and Elijah would ride along with me." His lips turned up in the sideways grin she'd never been able to resist.

But this time, she had to try.

She studied his face. He was sincere. He always was. But why?

She took a step back to think more clearly, but he didn't budge. She saw his reason, then, in his firm stance. He intended to be her bodyguard.

He hadn't stopped being Captain Beller, not completely. Maybe he never would. He wasn't trying to resurrect an old flame. He was protecting her because of what Elijah had told him about Phineas and because of the promise he'd made to Elijah.

But she wasn't as naïve as she'd once been. Seven years ago, she'd refused his offer of help, and those regrets were growing by the day.

The truth was, she was afraid of being left alone with Elijah in the evening while Mattie and Winston went to the schoolhouse to host the youngies and put up the greenery they'd be collecting for the Christmas Eve celebration.

She could go along with Mattie and Winston, but felt like she and Elijah would be totally out of place with a group of teenagers.

"That would be... fun. If you're sure you don't mind." She gave him a smile to hide her fear.

Only it wasn't Phineas she was afraid of right then. The reckless beat of her heart scared her more.

Hopefully, her heart would *rememberize* Mark was doing his duty—not offering a romantic second-chance.

Chapter Seven

Seated at the small writing desk under the bedroom window, Ellen heard the friendly tenor of Mark's voice coming from downstairs. Elijah giggled at something that had been said. Soon, their voices drifted away and the back door clapped shut.

Ignoring the butterflies in her stomach, she hooked the lock on her diary and slipped it into the single desk drawer. The sooner she joined them, the sooner reality would take its rightful place in her thoughts.

She hoped.

She'd been distracted all afternoon thinking about this sleigh ride with Mark. Fanciful, silly, and romantic notions plagued her, fueled by memories of their short-lived, secret courtship. She rolled her eyes at herself and pushed any hopes for a second chance with Mark out of her thoughts.

This was not a date. Besides the fact she had no reason to suspect that Mark still held any such affection for her, Elijah was coming along.

Downstairs, the house was empty. Mattie and Winston had already left, taking hot chocolate and sweet snacks to the schoolhouse where the young people would gather. Mark and Elijah must've gone to ready the sleigh, so she left to find them.

"There you are." Mark walked up just as she turned after closing the door. He was wearing camouflage trousers, a black parka, and a dark green ball cap. He certainly didn't look Amish.

"Is that what you wore in the Air Force?"

"No." He looked down at his outfit. "I wore camo fatigues on duty, but these aren't regulation. The only time I'll be wearing a uniform now is if they call me up for reserve duty."

"Oh." She really didn't know much about his life anymore. "Is that likely? That you'll get called back, I mean?"

He shrugged. "It's always possible. There's a lot happening in the world. Only God knows what's in store for me... for any of us, really."

"For sure." Only God knew what was going to happen in her life next as well. She stepped closer to him. "Did you... was it very hard... over there?"

A pained looked crossed his face, and she regretted asking.

"I'm sorry, it's none of my..."

He took her hand. He was wearing gloves. She'd forgotten hers. He must've noticed the moment she did because he reached for the other one and warmed them both in his.

"You can ask me anything, Ellen, and I'll answer as honestly as I'm able. Yes, it was hard. And sad. And terrible to see what evil men will do to others. But I get to come home to a prosperous and peaceful part of the world. What haunts me the most is knowing others are not so fortunate."

A lump welled in her throat. He'd go back. She knew he would, if he was called to aid others' suffering or to keep her part of the world at peace.

"I'm proud of you. Truly." She managed around the building tension in her heart at the thought of him leaving again.

He rested her hands against his chest and brought up his gloved hands to cup her face.

"Ellen," he said with enough warmth to melt the snow beneath them.

"Yes." Her eyes locked with his shining green ones.

She swallowed. Waiting. And though she'd been sure he wanted to kiss her, he stepped back.

When her hands dropped, he took one and tucked it in the crook of his elbow.

"Elijah is waiting for us."

That was all? And he said no more as they walked along to where Elijah was sitting patiently in the sleigh.

With care, Mark helped her up next to Elijah, so that her son remained between them when Mark entered from the other side. Of course, the middle was the safest place for a child to ride. Still, she was sure his motive had also been intentional to keep her at a distance. Suddenly, she didn't know if he'd really almost kissed her or she'd imagined it.

———

Mark wanted to kick himself all the way to... wherever it was he was going next. Halifax? Montreal?

What had he been thinking?

In that split second of time, when he'd lost his reason, he thought they were on the same wave-length. He'd seen in her expression an understanding of why he did what he did and why he might have to do it again.

I'm proud of you. Those sweet words were still ringing in his ears. They'd been his undoing.

Thankfully, he'd come to his senses before he began a kiss he wouldn't have wanted to stop. He didn't know which came as more of a surprise. That she'd appeared willing to kiss him. Or that he hadn't followed through.

For the first time since he'd seen her again, a spark of hope lit in his heart. Perhaps he'd misjudged her intentions. If she was proud of him, maybe she was more inclined toward a non-Amish way of life than he thought.

As they neared the schoolhouse, something unusual was happening around the side of the building. Mark eased the horse around the other way, but not before he heard raised voices and saw a group of men in a huddle. He recognized his own *datt*, first, then Joel, Winston, and his brother, Michael.

One glance at Ellen and he knew she found it suspicious too by the lift of her brows. He tethered the horse to a hitching post and helped Ellen from the sleigh.

Before helping Elijah, he whispered into her ear. "Maybe you and Elijah should go inside while I see what's happening?"

"*Ya*, it would seem so." She didn't make eye contact with Mark, but hurried Elijah out of the sleigh. "*Kumm*, Elijah. Let's go help *Tante Mattie*."

Once he'd seen them both safely through the door to the school, Mark made his way around to the sound of the commotion. Phineas' grating voice could be heard the loudest.

"Who do you Amish people up here think you are? No true Amish minister would keep a man from his own son. I'm taking Elijah back with me and you cannot stop me any longer." Phineas didn't sound inebriated this time, only angry and bitter.

"Ellen has not stated that you are the boy's father. And Elijah himself denies it." Mark's best guess was that statement came from Joel.

"Pah!" Phineas spat on the ground. "What does the child know? And the woman is a liar."

Mark was close enough now to see Winston clearly. His face was mottled red and his hands were fisted tightly behind his back.

"You have four daughters at home. Why are you not there caring for them? Because you are under the *Bann* is why. And that is for your own grievous transgressions for which you refuse to repent. You also have a wife, whom you married before Elijah was born. These are facts that do not lie." Winston wasn't yelling, but he looked fierce. "Nor do the bruises and broken bones my cousin received from your hand. Are you saying her mother and father also lied?"

Mark had heard enough. Too much, in fact. He should have put the pieces of this puzzle together ages ago.

"I believe I can settle this." Mark passed Winston and inserted himself directly in front of Phineas.

Before addressing Phineas, Mark looked each of the other men in the eye until his view rested on his *datt*. Herschel Beller held his gaze long enough to for Mark to know his father understood what he was about to do. And he wasn't going to try to stop him.

Mark had shared his desires with his *datt* years ago, as well as his heartache. The time had come to follow through.

Mark stepped closer to Phineas and held out his hand. "I'm Mark Beller."

Phineas snubbed the offer of a handshake. "I have nothing to say to you."

"Elijah is *my* son."

"And yet, he looks like me." A wicked smirk spread across Phineas' face.

"Really?" Mark scrutinized the man in front of him. "I don't think so."

Mark squared his jaw, willing the man to see the truth of the love Mark held for both Elijah and Ellen. That had to be enough to convince him.

Love was all Mark had.

When clearly, Phineas had none.

"How would your bishop feel about a quick little DNA test? That should settle the entire matter for good." It was a bluff. Mark knew he'd lose if he had to take a paternity test, and he'd never allow such evidence to exist, for Elijah's sake.

"Well?"

"I'll do no such sinful thing." Phineas switched in a flash from enragement to self-righteous hypocrisy. "I always knew she was a wh—"

Mark's fist landed straight in the man's gut. "Get out. And don't come back."

Chapter Eight

M ark watched his *datt* and brother walk out of sight as they led Phineas away from the school. Mark had warned Phineas that if he saw his face again, he had connections who could get Phineas a one-way ticket back to the States. And make sure he'd never be allowed to cross the border again.

He wasn't bluffing, and he planned to contact those friends, regardless.

Once they were well out of sight, Mark turned to Winston and Joel, who still stood by his side. "What I don't understand is what he sought to gain. Most men cover up that kind of sin and shame. Why is he here dredging it up?"

"You hit the right nerve, mentioning the bishop." Winston lifted his hat and ran his fingers through his hair. He was still calming down. "Phineas is not only in trouble with the church. The law is investigating him. He's hurt more women than Ellen, and some of them are pursuing legal action. He believed Ellen was the instigator and went after her to intimidate her. She came here for a safe haven... Now, I reckon he's just lost his mind. They call it mental illness, I think."

"*Nay*," Joel countered and rubbed at his temples. "It's called when your sins have eaten out your soul. If he won't repent, he'll have to pay the price as *Gott's* perfect justice sees fit to allow."

Mark shuddered. "So then, what was it that got him cuffed yesterday and back out here today?"

"They couldn't lock him up for walking down the street drunk, even though he was the likely cause of the accident. The driver had to swerve into the ditch to miss Phineas, but didn't see Amazon and Samy in the snow. Amazon dodged the car, but slipped and fell, which threw Samy."

"In the end, no one was injured too badly. They didn't have proof that Phineas had been the man in the road, but they've told him to leave the island on the first bus out tomorrow. Any hint of more trouble and they'll have him sent back to the States."

"Do they know about the legal case in the Pennsylvania?"

Joel didn't know.

Privately, Mark would make sure law enforcement got the information necessary to send Phineas back across the border to stay. For now, he didn't want to continue discussing what he thought should happen to Phineas.

No doubt, these men disapproved of the punch he'd given Phineas. Mark couldn't regret it, but he knew he was on thin ice with Joel.

Mark kicked a small stone.

Winston shoved his hands in his coat pockets.

Joel cleared his throat.

"Listen, I don't condone violence, even if a man has it coming. Lying either. But as for this business of you being Elijah's father... you could become his *datt*, well and truly. If Ellen were willing, of course."

Winston chuckled. "Yeah, I don't think that will be a problem."

Mark's head spun. Joel approved of Mark for Ellen? And Winston didn't think Ellen would object?

"Really?" Mark looked at Joel first. "After what just happened, you're trying to set me up with Ellen?"

"I've known you all your life, and you're a *goot* man. You may not have chosen our ways, but neither has she." Joel seemed to be letting that sink in.

Had Joel really just implied that Ellen hadn't chosen to be Amish, either? Mark was still working that out, when Winston interrupted his spinning thoughts.

"*Ya*, really, she'd more than happily give you a chance. And you'd make a great *datt*. Husband, too." Winston clapped Mark's back. "Course, seven years is a long time to wait. You probably shouldn't take too much longer. She might change her mind."

Joel choked back a snicker. "I believe I'll go see if Ellen will allow Elijah to come visit our place for a few hours. It's been a while since he and Owen have played together."

The minister winked at Mark, then turned to Winston. "Surely you can find some reason that Ellen would need Mark to take her on a ride? Some more greenery, perhaps?"

"*Ach*, did you see how much the *youngies* collected already?" Winston shook his head. "We definitely don't need more."

Joel shot Winston an exasperated stare.

"Oh." A slow dawning of Joel's intentions lifted Winston's mouth into a grin. "*Ya*, I can do that."

Chapter Nine

You could've told me.

I still thought it was my fault... and that I didn't deserve you.

They hadn't required many more words than those to sum up what had happened so long ago, and why. Ellen had watched Mark clear the pain from his face as best he could. She'd done the same. And they'd ridden together to his secret spot.

He'd wrapped a blanket around her shoulders and snuggled her close to his side—his nearness and warmth expressing more acceptance than words ever could.

Trees zipped past. They climbed and crested hills to soar down them as the sleigh's runners sliced through the icy snow. Each bump, every sway, the highs and then the lows, all converged like the passing years. The moments they'd missed. Lost. As if in one swift ride, all was forgotten to bring them together in the present.

Now they snuggled together under the same blanket, high on a tree-stand, staring at the stars.

"If you want to prosecute him, I'll support you."

"I want Elijah to have a peaceful life. If I get a summons to witness, then I'll go and tell the truth. It's not that I think he shouldn't face justice for what he's done... I just don't want to go back. This is home."

"With the Amish... in New Hope."

"Not just the Amish." She understood why he'd think so. After all, that was her excuse for turning him down years ago. "They've given me a place to start over, but I don't intend to join the Amish church."

"So you really don't?" He looked pointedly at her *kapp* and dress. "Up until a conversation with Joel and Winston earlier, I assumed you already had. Of course, it didn't make sense—not with the nursing degree and your other clothes. I couldn't figure it out—or I was just afraid to hope."

"I took the money you gave me and went to school." Ellen pivoted to be able to see him better. "My parents weren't supportive at first, but when Elijah came along, their hearts changed. I lived on my own after graduation. I dress this way here out of respect for Winston and Mattie while Elijah is staying with them. In Pennsylvania, I dressed this way out of respect for my parents when we were at their home."

"I see. It's decent of you." He glanced back at her. "You're beautiful in scrubs or an Amish frock. Makes no difference to me. I always thought you could do whatever you had a mind to do, Ellen. I'm proud of you as well."

"Thank you." The warmth of his words comforted her. "It wasn't easy, at home, but I was making do. Until Phineas…" She wasn't sure what else to say. The sincerity of the compliment truly touched her. She found his hand and held it, instead of searching for more words.

He didn't seem to mind.

"I think I can put the rest together." He was scowling again, much like he'd been when Joel and Winston had sent her out of the schoolhouse to find him.

She squeezed his fingers to bring his thoughts back to the here and now.

"So, what is it you want now?" He repositioned so that his full attention was on her. "I'll be honest. I'm trying to figure out how I can work my way into those plans."

Ellen leaned forward and lay her head on his shoulder. Looking back up at the starry night, she answered, "I'd like that."

Two days before Christmas, Mark bought a car to get him around the island, as well as back and forth to Halifax for a meeting with his potential new employer later in the afternoon.

"I filled her up for you." Dan King's son, Ethan, thumped the hood of the used mid-size SUV. "It's been an excellent vehicle. Mom just doesn't want to maintain more than one vehicle since Dad passed. And this one reminds her too much of him."

Mark had been sorry to hear of his former neighbor's passing. Dan King had been providing rides for the Amish in New Hope ever since they'd settled in the area. The King family had farmed this area for generations but welcomed the Amish with open arms.

"Dan was a fine neighbor to my family." The Beller's dairy shared a border with the King's land. "It will be an honor to drive his car, especially knowing the care he always took with his vehicles."

Ethan handed the key fob to Mark.

"Listen," Ethan scratched the back of his head, then continued. "There's also a chance a couple of acres will go up for sale soon. If you've a mind to keep a place near your kinfolk, there's no one my family would rather it go to more. Probably won't take long for someone to snatch it up. But if you're interested... well, I can make sure you know first."

Mark was already running late. He'd had to wait for the law office in Montague to open, so he could get the title transfer notarized. And he was supposed to pick up Ellen and drop her off in Montague on his way to Halifax. His hurried inclination was to decline Ethan's offer with a polite *no, but thanks for thinking of me.* That's exactly what he would've done just a few days ago.

But on second thought, he considered that this could be God's provision. If things went as he hoped with Ellen, Mark could build a nice home for them here.

As if sensing Mark's indecision, Ethan continued. "Dad was a veteran, too. And we think that if he knew a section of our family land was going to another veteran to help mom's finances, he'd approve. He'd more than approve, if he knew it was you."

"That's quite an honor, Ethan." Mark kicked at a leaf that had blown into the driveway. "I don't really know what to say right now. Let me think about it and get back to you. I've got your number."

"No worries. I know you're in a bit of a rush this morning, so you better get on. Nothing's going to happen before Christmas. You've got time to think it over."

Mark shook Ethan's hand, who reciprocated with a solid grip. "Thanks for thinking of me."

Not having to stop for a fill-up saved time, but when Mark turned into Winston and Mattie's drive to get Ellen, his brother-in-law flagged him down. Mark pulled to a stop and rolled down his window.

"She just left in a taxi." Winston bent down to speak through the window. "She was afraid she'd be late for her interview."

"I get it." Mark tried to keep his disappointment from showing. "I'll still head that way. If the timing's right, maybe she won't have to pay for a ride back, at least."

Kings County Memorial Hospital wasn't far by car, and Mark found the associated pediatrician's office easy enough. He walked into the waiting room right when Ellen was called back for her interview.

He gave her a thumbs up.

She smiled back at him and waved, and he took a seat to wait for her. If she was done in less than an hour, he could still make it to Halifax in time for his meeting.

His phone buzzed with a text.

Can we do a virtual meeting instead? CEO's flight is delayed.

No problem.

How about in five minutes?

Okay.

Mark got up and tapped on the receptionist's window.

She swiveled around in her chair to face him. "May I help you?"

"I'm with Ellen Miller. She just went back for an interview. When she comes out, would you please let her know Mark is outside waiting for her?"

"Sure." She made a note, and Mark thanked her.

Thirty minutes later, Mark was shutting down his laptop and saw Ellen emerge from the office. Realizing she wouldn't recognize the car, he jumped out and waved at her.

He couldn't tell from her expression if the interview had gone well or not.

"How'd it go?" He opened the door for her.

She paused before getting in. "I probably won't know until after Christmas. They have several candidates."

"But you must be the best." He thought she was for sure.

"I guess we'll see." She shrugged. "I thought you had to go to Halifax. Are you sure you have time to take me back?"

"It got changed to a web meeting. That's what I was doing out here on my laptop. Just finished. I'll tell you about it on the way."

Mark procrastinated the conversation with small talk. He wasn't sure how she'd take the news and hadn't figured out how to accept it himself yet.

"Ellen..." He really didn't want to tell her, but he couldn't keep it from her. "They rescinded the job offer. The company in Halifax is down-sizing." He didn't need to tell her that left only Montreal as an option for him.

And she didn't have to tell him what he already knew. Moving Elijah to a big city wasn't how either of them imagined this working out.

"Still, that doesn't mean that you won't be able to keep your promise to Elijah. Hopefully, this job works out for you and..." He thought of the parcel of land Ethan was offering to sell to him. "You'll be close to Elijah after Christmas, just like you promised. And that's what matters, right?"

"If this job comes through. But otherwise, I'll still be working in Halifax." She barely squeaked out the final words. "And it will be even worse than before because you'll be in Montreal." She hiccupped and then sniffed.

"We've gotten through worse." The words had seemed comforting before he actually said them.

There wasn't much else to say, and a minute later, he turned into his sister's driveway and stopped near the house.

"Thanks for bringing me back." She offered him a weak smile and pulled on the door handle.

He reached across to squeeze her other hand. "I'll still see you both at the Christmas Eve celebration tomorrow. Don't give up yet."

"You're right." She released her hold on the door and turned to face him. "Elijah has two speaking lines for his part as the angel. Remember, 'Fear not.' He told you that one. But the other is to Mary at the beginning." Ellen flashed a more natural smile at him, and her eyes brightened. "'For with God nothing shall be impossible.' We should *rememberize* that."

"Yes." Mark laughed at the word Elijah had made-up before. "We should."

Chapter Ten

If Elijah hadn't been in the Christmas program, Mark couldn't have paid attention at all. Probably wouldn't have come. He'd have stayed home and helped Michael with a sick cow.

Sure, he loved his sister, Mattie, and this would be her seventh and final Christmas Eve celebration as the teacher for New Hope. Most girls quit teaching when they got married. Like a true Beller would, Mattie did things differently and kept teaching all this time.

She and Winston hadn't been able to have children, but she'd decided to work full time at the maple farm, expanding their business. Tonight, she'd announce her replacement. She'd kept the secret from them all, Winston too. Other than Mattie, only the school board knew, and even they were remaining remarkably tight-lipped.

Still, Mark was here for Elijah tonight. And for Ellen, of course. Very much for her.

Elijah came on stage, which was really just the front of the one-room schoolhouse where the teacher's desk had been moved to the side. The room was set up like a church service, with men on one side and the women on the other.

Mark glanced across the aisle to find Ellen.

She was giving him a side-ways look, too. His heart flipped and he couldn't help but smile. The day before had been discouraging, but that look included him in a special moment.

Like a mother and father might share.

He had good news, but she didn't even know it yet. And yet she'd joyously connected with him across a crowded and dimly lit room. She hadn't given up.

Neither would he. Never again.

"For with Gott nothing shall be impossible." Elijah's line rang out boldly.

Mark's courage was bolstered.

Tonight, indeed, an impossible dream might very well come true.

———

Ellen was about to burst. She could hardly wait to tell Mark about the message the doctor's office left for her.

And she wasn't the only one. The entire room felt about to explode with discussions about the teacher who was taking Mattie's position in the next term. Michael Beller was conspicuously absent—something about a cow down. Out of all six brothers, she found it rather convenient for Michel to be the one left behind to doctor a cow.

The New Hope Amish had never had a male teacher. No one even remembered such a thing happening in Ontario, either, before they came to

Prince Edward Island. Ellen had heard of some Amish in the States employing male teachers, but it was a rarity. But the school board had chosen Michael, and tongues were trilling with the news.

A gentle tug encouraged her to turn around.

"Can we slip outside for a minute?" Mark asked.

She scanned the room for Elijah. He was with friends and would be occupied until time to leave. "Okay."

She followed Mark onto the small porch, then he held out her coat so she could slip it on.

"How about a walk? We won't go far. We can see the school from the front porch of Lydia's shop at the top of the hill."

She agreed. No one would be there tonight, and they could sit in the rocking chairs. It would be the perfect place to tell him her news.

As they walked the short distance up the hill, her hand fit securely into Mark's as if made to belong there. A light flurry of snow drifted down as they stepped across the road to Lydia's Amish Shop.

Mark brushed a few flakes of snow from one of the rockers for her to sit, but she wanted to tell him first.

"I have some good news."

They'd both spoken at the same time.

"Ladies, first." He stepped further under the covered porch and tugged at her elbow to come with him. "Or do you want to sit?"

"*Nay*... no, I mean. I rather like standing like this." And from his smile, he liked the nearness as well. "The doctor's office left a message this afternoon. They offered me the job here on the island."

"That's great, Ellen." Which, of course, she expected him to say. He'd never ask her to go with him to Montreal. He wanted what was best for her and Elijah.

"But I'm not going to take it."

"You should."

"*Nay*... no." She was trying to remember to use English more. "What I should do is whatever it takes to be with you. That's what is best for me and Elijah. He needs a family. And I need... you."

"Ellen, you don't have to. That's what I wanted to tell you." He was holding both of her hands now, making it hard to think straight.

"But you haven't let me tell you the full message. They also have an opening in Montreal. The choice is mine."

He put her hands on his chest, painfully reminiscent of the way he'd done before *not* kissing her.

"Don't do that."

"What?"

"Don't do that and *not* kiss me."

He laughed and cupped her face in his hands. Still *not* kissing her, he touched his forehead to hers. Frustrating man.

"I bought a piece of land. Two acres, to be precise, and guess what's right in the center of them?"

Baffling man. "I give up."

"Our tree."

"Our tree?" Her heart raced. "The one here?"

He touched the tip of his nose to hers. "The job in Montreal has agreed to let me work remotely, as long as I come to the office once a month."

"With God... nothing shall be impossible." Somehow, she squeaked out the words on what felt like her final breath.

And then, Mark's lips *almost* touched hers. "Want to build a proper house? I don't think the three of us can fit in the tree stand."

"Mark..."

"Hmmm..."

"Stop talking."

Finally, he did.

The man she loved kissed her.

And for a gloriously long and proper while.

Epilogue

E lijah knew June would forever be his favorite month of the year.

Of course, he liked June a lot, anyway. He had ever since he started going to school. But this June brought something better than the last day of school.

This year his *mamm* got married. And now he had a *datt*—the kind he'd prayed so hard for. *Ya, Gott* answered his prayers. Every. Single. One.

And Elijah didn't even mind how long *Gott* seemed to take getting around to it.

Becoming Elijah Beller was worth the wait.

Dear Reader,

That's one Beller brother down. Five more to go! I hope you've enjoyed Mark and Ellen's happily ever after in this Christmas novella.

Michael Beller is the next brother up for true love in New Hope. **Amish Dreams on Prince Edward Island, Book Five** (a full-length novel) is on its way.

New title and cover coming soon! More on that in my newsletter. Sign up at www.amygrochowski.com

Can't wait to see you there!

Blessings,

Amy

More from Amy...

View all of Amy's books in the Amazon store

Or visit

AmyGrochowski.com